CAMP KIDS

AND

SERPY'S WILD ADVENTURE

DIVE INTO ANOTHER CAMP KIDS BOOK...

BOOK 1

CAMP KIDS

AND

THE UNDERWATER ADVENTURE

...

BOOK 3

CAMP KIDS

AND

THE TREASURE MAP

CAMP KIDS

AND

SERPY'S WILD ADVENTURE

WRITTEN & ILLUSTRATED
BY SHARON SWAIN

PUBLISHERS NOTE: This is a work of fiction. Although places in this book may be real; names, characters and incidents are either the product of the author's imagination or are used fictitiously.

Cover design by Jonn Griffin and Sharon Swain

Published by:
Stone Fence Publishing
Burnt Hills, NY, 12027
USA

Printed in the United States of America
ISBN: 978-0-9827847-1-6

www.stonefencepublishing.com

FOR MY CAMP KIDS,

COLIN AND SOPHIE,
AND THEIR COUSINS HARVEY, OLIVIA, EDIE, GRIFFIN, AND DANTE

THANK YOU
MARK, JONN, GEORGETTE, ABBY, KAREN, KRISTIN, AND SUSAN

CONTENTS

CHARACTERS

Name: Grace Sophia Galley
Jobs: second grader, little sister to Cole
Interests: reading, writing, drawing, acting
Quote: "Hold on, let me just write that down."

Name: Colin (Cole) Mark Galley
Jobs: fourth grader, big brother to Grace
Interests: soccer, video games, surfing (but I haven't been yet)
Quote: "Awesome. Yep, that about sums it up, awesome."

Name: Julia Anne Morgan
Jobs: second grader, stuffed animal collector, aspiring cook
Interests: anything new and hip
Quote: "Just write the company, tell them they're old news!"

Name: Jacob (Jake) Holden Leftwich, III
Jobs: fourth grader, quarterback
Interests: surfing, football, basketball, golf
Quote: "Dude, just watch me."

Name: Olivia Gabriella Finn
Jobs: fourth grader, big sister to Harvey
Interests: diving, swimming, water colors
Quote: "Well come on, let's check it out!"

Name: Harvey Gabriel Finn
Jobs: third grader, little brother to Olivia
Interest: swimming and Dr. Who
Quote: "Just ask the animals, they'll know what to do."

Name: Carmine Dante Ubriaco
Jobs: second grader, self proclaimed dragon hunter
Interests: mythology (it's all real) and reptiles
Quote: "When I make it to Atlantis, I will be home!"

Name: Mikey Griffin Rosbottom
Jobs: kindergartener, little brother to Carolyn
Interests: rap, the club, being big
Quote: "If Cole likes it, I like it too."

Name: Carolyn Edith Rosbottom
Jobs: second grader, big sister to Mikey
Interests: tennis, candy, gymnastics, candy
Quote: "You guys are sooo weird."

CAMP KIDS

AND

SERPY'S WILD ADVENTURE

CHAPTER 1
COUSINS

"Mom, will you braid my hair for me?" Grace asked, rubbing her eyes as she walked into the camp's living room.

The camp was small, but Grace and her older brother Cole spent most of their time outside in the summer. So, they only really noticed how small it was when all of their cousins came to stay. This happened every summer for the week starting on the Fourth of July, and that was today. Carolyn and Mikey would be arriving any minute. Carmine's parents had called to say they had gotten a late start, so they would be another hour or so. Grace and Cole had always really looked forward to this week. But this year, they had other things on their minds.

"So, are you excited for tennis?" Mrs. Galley asked as she began to brush through Grace's long red hair. Grace liked to keep her hair braided or in a ponytail so that it didn't fall in her eyes while she was trying to read or write in her journal. It was also very helpful now that she was spending so much time swimming underwater.

"Yeah, I guess. Ow, that hurts," Grace complained, pushing some of the still loose hair from her big brown eyes. She had been so excited when she found out that the Beach Club would be offering tennis lessons to eight year olds this year, but now she was wishing that she could just swim all day.

"I hope Carolyn remembers her tennis racket. Does Julia have hers?" Mrs. Galley asked, twisting the band at the bottom of the first braid. "I'm surprised you girls haven't asked to go practice at the club."

"Yeah, I guess we've just been having so much fun swimming," Grace said, smiling up at her mom.

"I'm sure you'll have fun at tennis too. And you'll still have all afternoon to swim." Mrs. Galley kissed Grace on top of her head. "You're done. Now go wake up your brother, your cousins will be here any minute."

"Thanks, Mom," Grace said, heading off into the bedroom that she and Cole shared.

Grace turned sideways to get past the cots and air mattresses that had been set up for her cousins. She looked at the map that she and Cole had hung on the wood paneled wall of their camp bedroom. The map was old and it had handwritten notes on it. Cole was planning to add his own notes today, when he got back.

The map was unusual. It was of hills and valleys and rivers, but they were all underwater. It was a map of the Adirondack Waterways, or better said, the Adirondack *Under*waterways.

Cole and Grace and their camp friends, Jake and Julia, had found the map, along with lots of other underwater information in their clubhouse. They had been using the fire pit at an old abandoned cabin as their clubhouse for years. But, just last week they found the key to the cabin in the bottom of the lake, in a car. The lake is deep, very deep, and even though the kids had always known the car was there, they'd only just discovered a way to swim to it.

"Mornin'," Cole yawned from the top bunk. He rubbed his sleepy blue eyes and tried to comb his fingers through his shaggy blond hair. "Too bad you can't come with us today."

"Oh. I'm glad you're up. You know, I was thinking," Grace began, putting her hand to her neck and playing with the small pouch that was hanging there, "you guys better be careful today. You know Dad's still talking about that sea monster, and I know he thinks it's funny, but you never know. Here, look at the picture." Grace showed Cole the newspaper, where for the second week in a row the front page article was about a sea monster that had been seen in the Adirondacks. It showed a long neck coming out of the water. It was kind of blurry like it was taken from far away.

"That's a fake. We're only planning to go to the Chain Lakes anyway, and Olivia and Harvey were just there yesterday. Even if you girls aren't there, I think we can handle it," Cole stated, jumping down from the bunk and pulling a pair of swim trunks from his drawer. "We won't be going anywhere anyway, unless Jake and I find a way to get away from Mikey and Carmine.

Grace picked up a small, shiny leather pouch that was hanging on the bed post. The leather was covered with a tiny layer of smooth iridescent hair. It caught the light and played with shades of green and blue, making the pouch itself look like a miniature mountain lake in the palm of Grace's hand.

The stones that the kids were keeping in their necklace pouches held the magic that had started their summer adventure. While they were looking for fairies in the woods, Cole, Grace, Jake, and Julia, had found the glowing stones instead. They soon realized that the stones allowed them to breathe, see, and stay warm underwater. And better yet, never more than one minute passed above water, no matter how long they had been exploring underwater. So, their parents never worried and they could travel as far away as they wanted.

But that's not all. After finding the key to the clubhouse in the car at the bottom of the lake, they discovered that they were water sprites. In the books and journals they found in the clubhouse, they learned that there had been other water sprites in the woods before them, including some of their own relatives. They found out that water sprites have helped to protect water animals and the waters of the world for, well, like forever. They also found out that the magic powers of the stones only lasts while they are young, but they had decided not to worry about that yet.

Grace looked up at Cole and tossed him the stone. "You won't be going anywhere without your fairy stone either."

"I still can't believe that we found these awesome things and that we only just met Harvey and Olivia. It seems like we've known them forever. It's so cool that they're water

sprites too," Cole said, taking a deep breath. "This has already been the best week of my life. We know every inch of this lake except what's behind that old blocked-up river channel. And now that we know how to get to Brantingham, we can totally explore that lake too. Who knows maybe we can even go farther."

"They're here!" Mrs. Galley called from the other room.

Cole pulled a shirt over his head. "We might even make it to Scotland to see Nessy. Now go greet our cousins so I can get dressed!" he demanded, pushing Grace out of the room.

CHAPTER 2
THE DAY BEGINS

"See ya. Have fun at tennis, you two," Cole said, giving Grace a knowing look and waving to Carolyn.

"Take this, in case you need it when you're swimming," Grace said, handing a journal to Cole. "I've drawn some new maps. I thought you might want to take a look."

"Thanks," Cole smiled, taking the journal. "But like I said, I think we can handle it." He went to set the journal on the table, but Grace gave him such a look that he quickly shoved it into the back of his shorts. "There, I've got it. Happy now?"

Grace smiled and nodded.

Carolyn gave them both a funny look. “Maps? What do you need maps for? The lake is right there.” She pointed out the picture window that faced the small mountain lake, not fifty feet away, and added, “What’s it say, Pleasant Lake straight ahead?”

Cole didn't get a chance to answer because Carolyn's mom walked in.

"Here's your water bottle," Auntie Lorraine said, handing the bottle to Carolyn and then turning to Grace. "Take off that necklace Gracie. It keeps getting tangled in these gorgeous braids. It won't do you any good bouncing around at tennis either."

Grace's hair was the kind that people couldn't help but notice. It had tons of different shades of red, bits of blond, and even brown mixed in.

"Um, okay," Grace said, reluctantly taking off the pouch and clutching it in her hand. She had not taken off her fairy stone since she had first put it on in the clubhouse, that first day as a water sprite just over a week ago. She had no intention of keeping it off now either, but she found that it's usually easier to just listen to adults, and Auntie Lorraine didn't say she had to leave it off.

Mrs. Galley came into the camp. "Hurry up, girls. You're going to be late for the first lesson. Julia's waiting in the car so grab your rackets and let's go."

Grace ran to the back of the camp and reached for her tennis bag that was hanging on a peg outside the bathroom. It was tangled up with Cole's bag. She hung her necklace on an empty peg so she could use both hands to untangle the bag. When she finally freed it, her water bottle fell out and landed at her feet, just as she heard her mom call, "Don't forget to fill your water bottle!"

Grace picked up the bag and the bottle and ran to the kitchen. She filled up the water bottle, tucked it into her bag, and ran out the door.

****

"Cole, Cole, watch me dive," Mikey shouted, jumping from the dock. His hands were together in diving position, but the rest of his body was stuck in a cannonball. He had not left Cole's side since he arrived. He had even curled up on the couch next to Cole this morning, not giving him any time to look at the maps of the new lakes.

The boys had been playing King of the Dock and even though Cole and Jake had tried lots of times to jump in the water alone together, Carmine and Mikey always seemed to be there. So, when Mikey suddenly needed to go back to camp to use the bathroom, Cole decided to try out a new plan.

"Carmine, take my hand, I want to show you something before Mikey gets back." Cole took his cousin's hand and they walked to the edge of the dock.

"Don't do it, dude. Remember what Olivia said, it doesn't work for other people," Jake warned, shaking his head and watching Cole.

"We're family and he's the right age, eight, just like Grace and Julia. I think it'll work." Cole looked at Carmine.

Carmine looked back and forth between the boys with his inquisitive gray eyes, not sure he wanted to be a part of their experiment. "Hey wait a minute, what're you going to do to me?" Carmine pulled his hand out of Cole's. "Is there a turtle down there or something?" He asked, looking into the water. His jaw dropped. He pointed at Loony and Coolcat who were waiting, somewhat impatiently just under the surface of the water. "Wow, look at those guys!"

"Yeah, we know. That's part of what I want to show you," Cole said, bending down and patting Loony on the head. The loon and catfish were Cole and Jake's water guides, always swimming with them and helping to guide them through their new underwater world.

Carmine continued to stand on the dock with his mouth open, looking in disbelief, when he saw a gigantic bull frog swimming to join Loony and Coolcat. "Look at him. He's awesome. I bet I can catch him."

Cole and Jake knew that this would be their chance. Carmine loved catching frogs, and if he was with them, and it worked, he wouldn't even notice that he was underwater for longer than normal. Cole took Carmine's hand again and they jumped in after the frog. Carmine looked like a frog himself, with his long skinny arms and legs splayed out for his jump.

Jake dove in right behind them, but just before he went under, he heard Mikey call out, “Wait for me!”

Jake looked up toward the surface and saw Mikey climbing up the ladder onto the dock and then jumping back in. Mikey kept on swimming deeper and deeper, heading straight for Jake. Jake didn’t want to lose Cole and Carmine, but he couldn’t leave the kid. Mikey would probably keep swimming until he passed out or something.

Jake slowed down and he was right, Mikey kept swimming. When he got close enough, Jake saw that he was still wearing his life jacket. And as Mikey managed to swim impossibly deep, Jake saw that he was glowing, and it all started to make sense. “Where did you get that?” he asked, pointing to the pouch around Mikey’s neck.

CHAPTER 3
MIKEY!?!

"I found it, it's mine!" Mikey held onto the pouch. He was so determined to keep his find that he did not even notice that he was at the bottom of the lake, bubbles flowing out of his mouth with each word.

Jake laughed to himself, thinking that it must be great to be five. All of a sudden being ten seemed very old. "It's not yours. It's Grace's, she must have forgotten it. Where did you find it?" Jake realized that even though it was Grace's stone, it did seem to be working for Mikey.

Carmine was fine too. He and Cole were holding hands and swimming toward Mikey and Jake. Carmine held the giant bullfrog in his other hand and was talking the whole time, bubbles drifting to the surface.

"It was by the bathroom. Finders keepers, losers weepers. That's what Carolyn always says," Mikey said with his hands on his hips and a determined look on his face. He was ready for a fight. Then he saw Cole and Carmine. "Hey, what're you guys doing here?"

“Us? What are *you* doing here? And why do you have Grace’s fairy stone?” Cole shouted, ready to drag Mikey back to the dock and take the pouch. But then Mikey looked at him with his giant eyes.

“It’s not Grace’s, it’s mine. I found it fair and square! And I’m not leaving either.”

Cole let out a huge sigh. “Well Jake, I guess we’re all going to the Chain Lakes. But, Mikey, you have to give it back as soon as Grace gets home.”

“Why? Where are the Chains?” Mikey asked, looking around, finally realizing where he was. “Hey, where are we anyway?” He looked left and right and then he slowly looked up toward the surface. “Oh no, I’m underwater, I’m going to drown! This life jacket stinks!” Mikey pulled at his life jacket. It was making him float just slightly off the lake bottom, like he was walking on the moon. “Help me, Cole, help me!” Mikey screamed, swinging his arms and legs around like a mad man, bubbles floating everywhere.

"Calm down, buddy. It's all right. We can breathe down here. It's all right." Cole tried to control Mikey with his one free arm.

Jake stepped up and grabbed Mikey. "Chill out, dude, we know what we're doing. It's a clubhouse thing and you're old enough to join this year, so just chill out!" Jake knew that these were key words.

Mikey had been desperate to join the club for the last few years but he'd been too young and all he did was cause trouble.

Mikey stopped flailing and looked at the three boys. "Really, I'm old enough? This is what you guys do when you're part of the clubhouse?" he asked, looking up at the older boys with his big brown eyes. His moppy dark hair was flowing around his face. He'd worked all year to grow his hair just like Cole's. He was very proud.

Carmine giggled. Cole had already explained the whole story to him. And Carmine being Carmine, didn't even question it. It was like he was expecting to be told that he could breathe underwater and travel from lake to lake through underwater rivers. He was even determined that his new frog friend was his animal guide.

"Yeah, Mikey, this is what we do in the club. And this is my club animal." Carmine held up the frog for Mikey to see. "His name is Blue Dog."

Now Mikey laughed. "Blue Dog? But he's a frog.

You're so silly, Carmine." Mikey laughed again. It was a deep laugh, more suited for an eighty-year-old man than a five-year-old boy.

"Enough of the small talk, we have to meet Harvey," Cole said. "Mikey, don't lose Grace's pouch, and stay close. Carmine, you have to hold onto my hand the whole time. Don't let go or the fairy stone won't work. Jake, you'd better take the back of the line."

Cole tugged Carmine and began swimming toward the river channel leading to Brantingham Lake. He moved a rock with the help of Loony, to block the crosscurrent. The boys rode the turbulent river of water through the small dark channel leading into the big lake.

"I'm gonna find a way to surf that channel by the end of summer," Jake said as he swam out and into the big lake. He had managed to stay upright this time, unlike his first attempt, when he and the other water sprites had been tossed and turned around and around in the channel.

"Wow! That was like being inside a hurricane!" Carmine shouted. He was smiling from ear to ear.

So was Mikey. Both boys were trying to get their balance after being tossed around by the current inside the channel.

"Let's do it again. That was fun!" Mikey squealed, turning to enter the tunnel again.

"Sorry, buddy, but not yet. We have other places to go." Cole looked at Jake. "You'd better take his hand. I think we might lose him if we're not holding on."

"Come on, Mikey," Jake grunted, pulling Mikey back out of the river channel and dragging him backward as he swam after Cole and Carmine.

The boys met up with Harvey and together they headed toward the Chain Lakes channel tunnel. Loony, Cole, Carmine with Blue Dog clutched in his hand, Harvey and his turtle Tink, Coolcat the catfish, Jake, and Mikey all in a line.

They looked like a glowing string of Christmas lights, gliding through the water.

When they got closer to the river channel opening, they felt the current start to pull at them. Mikey was so excited he let go of Jake's hand and tried to swim closer up to the front of the line of kids. Just as Cole entered the tunnel, Mikey caught up with Carmine. The two boys were pulled into the tunnel together.

Carmine continued to hold on tight to Cole's hand as they twisted and turned head over heels through the channel, knocking into Mikey with every turn. The current was stronger than the small channel and the kids had no control, they couldn't see anything. When they were all shot out at the other end, in the westernmost part of the Chain Lakes, Mikey was missing.

CHAPTER 4
SACANDAGA

"Wow, that current was so much stronger than the one from our lake. It was like a huge wave back home." Jake really missed California when he came to spend summer at camp with his grandparents and he was desperate to have a more challenging wave to ride. "Awesome, right, Mikey?" His smile quickly faded as he looked in each direction. "Uh, I think I mighta lost Mikey back there. Has anyone seen him?"

All of the boys looked around. Loony and Coolcat were already at the mouth of the river channel, swimming in frantic circles and looking between the boys and back into the darkness of the channel.

"Well, where could he have gone?" Jake asked innocently. "He pulled away from *me*. It's not my fault."

Harvey shook his head back and forth. “Oh no, there’s another tunnel in there,” he said. “I didn’t think about it, because with the current, I didn’t think you could get in it coming this way. And the animals have never let us anyway. It has this weird greenish glow.” Harvey looked very worried.

He and his sister Olivia had found their stones last summer, and they had traveled farther than the Pleasant Lake sprites. But this was his first time swimming without his older sister.

"There is *what*? Another channel in there? Where is it? We've got to go find him," Cole shouted, looking back into the darkness of the channel, panic stricken. "Harvey, how do we get back in there?"

But Harvey didn't have to answer. He and Jake were already following the animals back into the channel opening. Cole raced after them, dragging Carmine along.

They stayed toward the top, where the current was slow enough for them to stay in control. With the glow from their fairy stones they were able to clearly see the pressed mud and rock walls of the channel. Some sections were wide and high, and some sections were low and narrow. The boys swam for what felt like miles. Riding through the first time at the bottom of the channel was like riding a watery elevator at warp speed, but here at the top, this was more like riding a floating sidewalk. The distance felt much more real at this speed. Above water, it was at least forty miles to the Chain Lakes.

"There. It's right there," Harvey finally said, pointing ahead to a glowing green channel entrance.

Tink, Loony, and Coolcat stopped at the entrance, looking into the strange greenish glow. They kept diving into the water and coming back up to look at the boys. Blue Dog watched from the safety of the pocket of Carmine's swim shorts, where he was now tucked in. His long arms and head were sticking out the top.

"I think they're telling us that we have to dive into the river to catch the undercurrent," Harvey said, looking at Tink. "If you miss the current, who knows where you'll end up and then even more of us will be separated."

"Carmine, you're with me. Jake, you and Harvey hold hands so that at least there will always be two of us together. We'll meet you at the other side, wherever that might be." Cole looked at Carmine. "Are you ready? Dive down as deep as you can. And don't let go!"

The green glow surrounded them inside the channel. The current was even stronger but it took them even longer to make it through to the other end. They must be traveling even farther away. When they were tossed out into the lake, Mikey was still nowhere to be seen.

"What do we do now? We don't know where we are and we don't even know for sure if Mikey is here," Jake said, looking around for clues. "Ya know Mikey was always kind of a pain anyway. Would it be such a big deal if we didn't find him?"

"Oh, shut up!" Cole and Carmine both said at the same time.

Jake laughed. "Yeah, yeah, I was just kidding. But seriously if this all works out, I'm coming back here, that current was way awesome! And check out the green swirls. I feel like I'm in a test tube or something."

Cole just rolled his eyes. All he could think about was his lost cousin.

Harvey patted his turtle. “Tink, show us the way.”

Tink and the other animal friends began swimming toward the middle of the lake. It was a big lake, much bigger than the other lakes that the kids had been in. It was different than the other lakes, too, because there was a constant current pushing at them, almost like it was a giant slow-moving river, or maybe a reservoir. And there was that glowing green, drifting in streams of smoke through the lake. Slowly, the four boys followed the animals into the unknown waters.

Cole remembered the picture in the newspaper that Grace had shown him this morning. The sea monster in the news, she had said it was in a reservoir in the Adirondacks. He was wishing that he had paid more attention to Grace or even to his dad when he warned him last week. Then he remembered he had the journal Grace had given him before they left.

Cole slowed down and struggled to pull out the journal. He finally managed to get it out and fumbled through the pages until he found what he was looking for. Grace had written everything down, just as he knew she would. But it wasn't good news.

"I think I might know where we are," he shouted up to Jake and Harvey, swimming faster to catch up. "I think this is Sacandaga Lake. And if it is, there's been a huge sea creature here. It's been in the newspapers. People are really scared. It's been breaking docks and flipping boats. Mikey might be in even more trouble than we thought." Cole took a deep breath and continued, "And if this is Sacandaga Lake, then it's a reservoir, and a town was flooded to make the lake. Grace says the buildings and everything are still down here."

"Dude, my grandpa was just talking about that sea serpent this morning. He thought it was a joke," Jake said, shaking his head from side to side. "We better find Mikey quick. Knowing him, he's already trying to fight the serpent, thinking it's a clubhouse game or something."

"Yeah, my parents were pretty freaked out about all this sea monster stuff on the news too. They told me I couldn't go swimming today," Harvey blurted out. "I had to sneak out to meet you guys."

All of the boys just kept swimming, following the animals and fearing what they might find. They passed old waterlogged trees, railroad tracks, toppled-over houses, rusted-out cars, and even swing sets. The swings were gently swaying with the current. They went up and over hills and down valleys, the whole time swimming against the slow current.

"All right, this is like straight out of a scary movie. I kkkeep thinking that it's gggoing to jjjump out at us," Jake stuttered, with an exaggerated stammer. He quietly swam up behind Carmine and flicked one of his ears and shouted, "Watch out!"

Carmine just shrugged him off and kept swimming.

"Well, I'd better just make sure you don't get lost, Carmine," Jake continued, grabbing at Carmine's hand.

"You don't have to worry," Carmine laughed, slipping his small hand out of Jake's grasp. "I'm sure he's friendly."

Jake stopped, hands on his hips, "Whatever, munchkin. I wasn't really worried. I was just trying to scare you." But, Jake's body tensed, realizing he was now falling behind. He quickly swam to catch up and wedged himself between Cole and Harvey, the eerie lake was getting the best of him.

CHAPTER 5
THE VILLAGE

"Look, up there. Do you see all of the lights?" Harvey asked, pointing into the distance ahead of them. There was a white glow above an underwater hill, like the lights of a city in the night sky, but twinkling and glimmering, not just glowing.

"Come on, swim faster. Let's check it out. If I know Mikey at all, I know he would head toward the lights." Cole swam faster, heading straight ahead, pulling Carmine behind.

As they got closer, they heard music and voices. They swam up to the top of the hill and looked down over a town. It was a glowing, glittering, sparkling town full of glowing, glittering, sparkling people and animals.

"No way! It must be a water sprite town. That's so awesome. Come on, let's check it out!" Jake called, swimming off over the hill, thankful to be near other people again. The other boys quickly followed.

They all stopped at the bottom and looked around. There was a hair salon, a flavored-ice parlor, a surf supply store, a popcorn-shrimp stand, and a boat repair shop. There were water sprites scattered here and there. They were all moving quickly and looking worriedly up toward the surface. They were dressed in all different types of swimwear, and the kids could hear lots of different languages being spoken.

There were specialty food stores and shops selling specialty diving equipment, GPS systems, and maps. There was everything a water sprite could ever want. And at the end of the village, there was a carnival.

"That's where Mikey will be," Carmine declared, pointing to the carnival with his spare finger. Blue Dog, now back in Carmine's hand, waved through the water as he moved.

There was a sea horse merry-go-round ride, a jellyfish bouncy-bounce, clown fish handing out blowfish balloons, and a hammerhead shark running a "strong man" booth. There were even mermaids. And at the very end there was a baby whale giving rides on his water spout.

"Hurry, let's go!" Cole yelled. Again the group of boys swam as fast as they could through the town toward the

carnival.

“Whoa!” Jake shouted, stopping. “What about that surf shop? He might be in there.” He pressed his hands and nose against the glass to get a better look in the shop window.

Harvey and Cole just rolled their eyes and kept swimming.

“There he is!” Cole yelled, spotting Mikey on top of the stream of water shooting out of the whale’s blowhole. He was shouting and waving his arms at the boys.

“Look at me! Look at how high I am!” Mikey yelled. He was still in his life jacket, floating on his belly on top of the whale’s geyserlike water spout.

"Get down here!" Cole shouted back. "We thought you were lost forever!"

"I wasn't lost. You were. I've been here having fun the whole time." Mikey hadn't even cared that he was alone in this new underwater world. When the whale ride was over he said good-bye to the whale, the merman in charge of the ride, the girl who was next in line, and the boy behind her. Then he said good-bye to the sea urchin that was collecting the tickets. Then he swam back down to Cole and the others.

"Your club is so great. Thanks for letting me join," Mikey sang with a giant smile. "Is this carnival always here?"

"I hope so. This is unbelievable," Harvey murmured, looking around, amazed. "Look at all the water sprites and ocean animals, and, and the mermaids." The last words came out slower and with a hint of a nervous giggle.

"Yeah, dude, that's what I was thinking," Jake said, drifting toward a group of mermaids that were heading in their direction.

Cole and Harvey followed right behind. Carmine and Mikey were trying to head toward the giant squid that had an eye bigger than Mikey's head, but they didn't get far because they were being dragged backward by Cole and Jake toward the mermaids.

"Hi," Jake stammered. It was all he could get out. His tongue seemed to be caught at the back of his throat.

"Hello," the three mermaids said in unison. "First time to the carnival?" they asked.

"Yes." Again, only one word making its way out. Jake shook his head up and down to be sure he was understood.

Cole and Harvey also shook their heads, mouths dropping open and little bubbles escaping. Carmine and Mikey were turned backward watching a tiger shark that was slowly swimming past.

"This is our third year. Terrible this year, though, must be the carnies were afraid. We plan to head home tonight. We wouldn't want to be caught here with that wild serpent on the loose." Again the mermaids spoke, their voices melding together into one singsongy chorus.

"What do you mean wild?" Cole asked, getting his thoughts back and remembering the newspaper article.

"Oh, you didn't hear? There's a sea serpent here somewhere. It's causing all sorts of trouble. It wrecked the campsites and it stole all of the Mediterranean seaweed that was brought in for the carnival feast." The mermaids told the story quickly, like they did not want to be caught saying anything bad about the serpent.

"Is he dangerous?" Cole asked.

"Well no, not normally, but this one seems angry. They say he would eat you whole if you got in his way. If you're smart, you would leave too." The mermaids waved to the boys and took off toward the campsite.

CHAPTER 6
SEA SERPENT?

"But he's not mean," Mikey whined, pulling on Jake's arm, trying to get his attention. "I met him on my way here."

"What?!" Cole, Harvey, and Jake all yelled, staring at Mikey.

"Yeah, he was sleeping when I came into the lake. I wanted to pet him, and he opened his eyes, but then he just closed them again." Mikey acted like this was a completely normal experience, meeting a napping sea monster while endlessly breathing underwater.

Carmine's gray eyes lit up. "I bet he's right, sea monsters aren't mean. They're just big. I've read about them in all of my books. I'm going to Scotland to see Nessy sometime," he added, shaking his head up and down. "I wonder how this one got here. The river channel we came through would be way too small for him." Carmine was stroking Blue Dog, and holding him a little too tightly. Blue Dog's eyes were bulging even more than normal for a frog.

"Good point, how did he get here?" Cole asked, opening Grace's journal. He flipped through a few pages. "Jake, remember when we were reading about the creatures of the Adirondacks in that book. There was that serpent in the big lake, what was his name Champy or something?"

"Oh, ummm, Champ I think. Yeah that's it, from Lake Champlain. Do you think that's him?" Jake asked, not stopping for an answer. "Maybe he's stuck here. Mikey, do you think you could find him again?"

"Wait, do you think it's safe?" Harvey asked with a funny look. "Olivia is going to be mad enough when she finds out we went into that green river channel, but if I get hurt she'll definitely be furious."

Carmine reached his Blue Dog hand over and rested it on Harvey's shoulder. "It's fine, they're not mean." Then he looked at the animal friends. "Blue Dog, Loony, Coolcat, take us to him." Carmine was right at home living in this underwater world. It was hard to believe he didn't have a fairy stone of his own.

Mikey pulled on Jake's hand, ready to follow Carmine before Jake and Cole could even decide if it was a good idea. Cole let Carmine drag him further into the lake until finally, helplessly shrugging his shoulder, Cole began to swim too. Jake and Mikey followed right behind.

"Well, wait for me. I'm not trying to get home by myself!" Harvey called, giving in and joining the line of shining kids and animals again as they swam together through the lake, toward what everyone else was swimming away from. They left the carnival behind somehow knowing that they, as water sprites, were meant to help this sea monster.

CHAPTER 7
SERPY

"Look there he is!" Mikey yelled, pointing up ahead to a group of hills.

When the kids swam closer, they saw a hill of green seaweed snuggled between two shrub-covered mounds. The hill looked a little out of place, but again Mikey was the only one that noticed it.

"Look, look, he's that one!" Mikey swam toward the seaweed hill.

The rest of the boys stopped where they were, watching as Mikey swam right up next to a bump in the seaweed at the top of the hill.

"Hi, it's just me again. I brought my friends." Mikey spoke to the sea monster like it was a puppy, petting his giant eyelashes. He stroked the lump of seaweed and a giant eye

opened right under his hand. Mikey climbed right up on the sea serpent's back, straddled the huge neck, and hugged him. The serpent opened its other eye and a big teardrop welled up in the corner, rolling out and down his cheek, clearing a streak in the seaweed. Underneath was his shiny, purple scale-like skin. It had a faint greenish glow. The same glow of the river channel.

"Oh no, what's wrong, Serpy? Can I call you Serpy?" Mikey asked, as he tried to lean forward to wipe the tear.

"What is it, little one?" Carmine asked, dragging Cole with him as he moved forward to stroke Serpy's big, yellowy-orange, elephantlike webbed toes. "We'll help you."

"Good idea Carmine. You and Cole can take care of this. Harvey and I will be staying way over here for backup," Jake said, helping to push Cole forward, as Carmine continued to pull at him. Jake then stepped back even farther away and moved behind Harvey, who just stood, staring at the giant sea monster, nodding in agreement.

Cole turned to Jake. "Real nice. You know, Jake, you can be such a jerk sometimes. It wouldn't hurt you to help, too, you know." Then looking at Carmine, Cole said, "I guess it's just us and Mikey. But what do you mean „little one'? You must be joking, this thing is ginormous!" As Cole spread his arms to help demonstrate how big the serpent was, he dragged Carmine with him. He created a line of little bubbles behind Carmine as he floated up and off the ground.

Jake and Harvey continued to stare back at Cole, not quite ready to trust Mikey's giant new friend.

"Cole, he's right here, and he's not a thing, he's just a baby. Sea serpents grow to be much bigger than this. Right, Serpy?" Carmine looked at the serpent waiting for an answer.

The sea monster blinked his eyes and gently shook his head up and down again. Mikey giggled, holding on tighter to the huge neck, looking like he was on a giant rocking horse.

"So you mean you're not Champ?" Cole asked, thinking about the book in the clubhouse that showed photographs of Champ from the 1920s. And that Mr. Ostrander, his teacher, told him about Henry Hudson seeing a sea monster. There's no way this could be the same one. He would be like a few hundred years old.

The sea serpent gently shook his head from side to side. The tears began to form in his eyes again, hanging for just a second on his long lashes, before rolling down his cheek. Cole looked back at Jake and Harvey. The boys were all silently wishing that Grace, Julia, and Olivia were with them. Cole didn't know what to do now. He couldn't just leave the big baby monster here all by himself, to be hunted down by the people above water. And now even all of the water sprites and other water animals from the carnival were afraid of him too.

Just then, Cole realized that Loony was using his wings to dust off the rest of the seaweed that Serpy had used as camouflage. Tink, Blue Dog (finally free of Carmine's grasp), and Coolcat joined Loony.

"What is it, guys?" Cole asked the animals. "What are we supposed to do?"

The animals continued to dust off Serpy. He slowly lifted his head and stopped crying. He turned and set Mikey on the ground. He had a big belly like an elephant, a long

thick tail, and with his neck stretched high he was as tall as a giraffe. He looked like a purple scaly brontosaurus with nostrils like a dragon. His whole body gave off that green glow. He slowly turned his head and looked at Carmine. His eyes told a story that only Carmine understood.

"He's lost," Carmine said. "He was playing with his mom when a black jellyfish came after them. Black jellyfish can make him very sick, so he and his mom swam away. But he got sucked into a river current when his mom tried to hide him in a tunnel opening. He could hear her yelling but she was too big to come after him. When he tried to get back through the channel, he ended up here. He doesn't know where he is and he doesn't know what happened to his mom."

Carmine stroked Serpy's knee and continued, "He was hungry, so he went looking for food but a fisherman saw him and yelled. It scared him so he tried to swim away, but the wave he made tipped the fisherman's boat over and broke some docks. It was just an accident. He was just scared and hungry.

"Then he went to the carnival to look for food, but he saw the black jellyfish again and so he hid in the seaweed. His waves accidentally ruined the carnival campsite and now even the water animals are scared of him. So he stole the seaweed and he has been hiding here ever since."

Mikey looked furious. "We've got to help him find the way back to where he came from." He snuggled into Serpy's neck and whispered, "We'll help you find your way home. Cole will know what to do."

Cole looked at Jake and Harvey again. "Um, yeah, we'll help. Right, guys?" Cole stated loudly, giving Jake and Harvey a stern look.

"Look in the book," Jake finally said, walking closer to Serpy. "Grace must have written something helpful."

"And ask the animals," Harvey suggested, coming forward, "they've always been able to help me and Olivia find our way home."

"Good idea," Cole said. "Um, I just want to see how big he is. Here, Mikey, hold Carmine's hand." Cole swam back behind Serpy and came around his tail with the journal open. He looked over the maps that Grace had drawn. "We just need to know how to get you back home." Cole turned to Loony, "Can you help?"

Loony proudly held his head high and took the journal from Cole. He swam up to Serpy and showed him the map, pointed at a few different things on the page and swam back to Cole. Loony handed Cole the journal and when he looked at the page, the map was glowing in a green light, highlighting the path that Serpy needed to take to get home to Lake Champlain.

CHAPTER 8
TO THE NEXT LAKE

Cole looked up at his friends. "All right boys, we need to get moving before anyone catches up with us. This little big guy is hungry and misses his mom, and thanks to Grace and Loony we can just follow this map." Cole waited until the others weren't looking and shoved the journal away again.

Mikey smiled and hugged the huge serpent's legs. Carmine joined in with a one armed hug. Serpy bent down to the boys and Mikey whispered in his ear, "See, buddy, I told you. My cousin Cole, he knows everything."

Serpy brushed his cheek gently against Mikey and Carmine, accidentally knocking them back. The boys laughed as Cole helped them up. Cole took Carmine's hand again.

After reminding Mikey how important it was to stay close, the whole crew took off in the direction of the river channel that would lead them to Lake George. They stayed close to the bottom and swam slowly, keeping a look out for humans above them on the lake.

"How much farther, Loony?" Cole asked after a few minutes of swimming.

Loony turned and stretched his wing out pointing ahead. Cole looked and saw that the current changed direction, making the seaweed sway toward a dark spot in a hillside instead of flowing down the lake. "That must be it."

"Watch out!" Jake yelled from the back of the line. Up above, a boat had stopped and a camera was being lowered into the water. It had a News Channel 6 logo on it. "They're looking for Serpy! We have to hide. Quick!"

Serpy turned, hearing his new name, knocking Cole, Carmine, and Harvey backward with his wake. They watched as the news camera was lowered right above Serpy's head.

"Dive! Go, go, go!" Cole yelled, pulling Carmine down toward the bottom of the lake.

Harvey, thinking quickly, swam toward the surface, and pulled the camera wire just before it fell in front of

Serpy's face. At the same time, he pushed on Serpy's head with his foot, forcing him to swim down.

"Down, Serpy! Go down! It's the people looking for you!" Serpy seemed to finally understand and dove down full force toward the bottom of the lake.

Harvey and the camera were both pushed by Serpy's wave. Harvey was pushed almost all the way up to the boat, which was swaying and rocking. He could hear the men on the boat shouting, as it threatened to tip over. The camera continued to swing back and forth under Harvey. He let go and swam toward the bottom, hoping it would not sway enough to get a glimpse of him, or even worse a glimpse of Serpy. But as he continued down, he heard someone shout, "Look there it is, I see its tail, and look at that moving light!! Pull up the camera! Let's get out of here!"

Jake shouted more frantically as the kids made it closer to the bottom. "Go farther, to that barn over there!"

Carmine and Cole made it to the water logged, dilapidated old barn. They pushed the heavy door open just enough for Serpy to fit through. Mikey swam in and Jake waited for Serpy and Harvey before he pulled the door closed.

"Wow! That was a close one. Good eye, Jake," Cole said, turning to his friend, "I sure am glad you decided to help out."

"No problem, dude, I do what I can," Jake drawled. He peeked out the barn door. "Hey they're taking the camera up."

"Yeah, they sounded pretty scared when they saw Serpy's tail, and I think my shining feet didn't help much either," Harvey laughed.

“We’d better get out of this lake,” Cole breathed. He was ready to get out of Sacandaga. He knew that soon they would have to worry about the sprites, merpeople, and animals leaving the carnival too. “Come on. Let’s get to that river channel.”

CHAPTER 9
ATLANTIS?

"It's all right, Serpy, we're almost to the next lake now," Carmine whispered. "You're not alone anymore. We won't let anything happen to you. We promise. Right, guys?"

"That's right. We've got your back," Jake added. He laughed watching Serpy nuzzle his head in closer to Carmine. "It's hard to believe anyone's afraid of you."

Mikey let go of Jake's hand, climbed onto Serpy's back and declared, "I'm going to ride up here. I have Grace's stone, so I don't need to hold your hand."

Serpy smiled and nodded his head just slightly.

Cole rolled his eyes and shook his head. "Well, I can't really say no now. But, Serpy, you'd better make sure he holds on."

Again, Serpy smiled and nodded his head.

Cole added, "And Mikey, you're still with Jake through the river channels."

Serpy, with Mikey on his back, followed the kids out of the barn door, which swayed, creaked once, and then slowly and quietly collapsed onto the lake floor.

"Is that it?" Cole asked, pointing ahead to an old stone tunnel, tucked in the dark spot of the hillside. It must have been a bridge when it was above water. "It looks so cool."

"Yeah, it's like an entrance to a castle," Carmine said, excited, "or maybe it's the entrance to Atlantis. In my book it said that there were stone arches that led travelers from the sea into the city of Atlantis. Maybe we're going to discover Atlantis." Carmine stopped swimming and stared off into the distance, a huge smile was on his face. Cole stopped with him.

"Sounds great, munchkin, but the sign on the bridge says this way to Lake George, so I guess you're out of luck," Jake laughed, rubbing Carmine's head.

"That doesn't mean anything! Maybe we have to go through Lake George to get to Atlantis," Carmine snapped, pushing Jake's hand off his head. "And don't call me that. I'm only two years younger than you and I'm not even short."

"Chill out, dude, it's just an expression." Jake rubbed Carmine's head again. "My dad just wrote to me about finding some sunken treasure. That's what he does on the weekends, ya know, he's a treasure hunter. I bet he knows about Atlantis." Jake scratched his head. "My grandpa said that my mom hated it when he went diving. She had been diving with him the day she left." He shook his head and cleared his throat. "When I get home, I'll look through his stuff and see what he knows about Atlantis."

Cole looked at Jake. He never talked about his mom. All that Cole knew about her was that she had left Jake and his dad when Jake was one and Cole had heard that from his own parents. Jake had never even mentioned her before. Cole, Grace, and Julia had decided they wouldn't bring it up either.

Harvey smiled, patting Carmine on the shoulder. "I think it would be so cool to find Atlantis too."

Serpy pushed through the middle of the boys who had all stopped to talk. He swam right past them and into the tunnel entrance. He turned to see if the boys were following.

"All right, Serpy, we're coming, buddy," Cole said, pulling on Carmine, snapping him out of his daydream. "Atlantis will have to wait for another day."

“It’s gonna be tight,” Jake said, swimming around Serpy to look at the tunnel opening. “Yep, it’s gonna be a close one.”

“You can do it, Serpy, just swim as fast as you can. We’ll be right behind you,” Mikey cheered.

“Right, sounds good. On the count of three, just blast through and we’ll be right behind you,” Cole said, holding tight to Carmine’s hand as they got in position behind Harvey. “Jake, hold on tight to Mikey!” Cole checked that his shorts were tight, tying his shorts string up to his fairy stone necklace just to be sure.

Carmine stuffed Blue Dog back in his pocket.

“Ready, one, two, three, swim!!!” Jake yelled, pushing on Serpy’s giant backside.

CHAPTER 10
STUCK

Serpy dove down headfirst into the undercurrent, paddling with his arms, kicking with his webbed feet, and disappearing in the darkness of the tunnel.

The boys swam with all their might, following the sea serpent into the dark channel water. It was hard struggling against the rough waves from the sea serpent's kicks. But as soon as they got some momentum and entered the tunnel, they caught the current and quickly sped up. That was until they crashed into one another and then into Serpy's enormous behind, which was tightly wedged between the sides of a narrow part of the tunnel. Serpy was wiggling and kicking and pushing to get free.

"Push him! We have to push him!" Jake yelled back to the others.

"He's gonna kill one of us with those giant feet," Cole screamed, pulling Carmine down just in time to avoid being kicked in the head.

"I can't *stop* pushing him. It's the current, it just keeps getting stronger," Harvey yelled, trying to hold onto the tunnel walls to avoid crashing into Cole.

"Dude, stop pushing me!" Jake shouted, trying to turn and push Carmine away.

"We can't move!" Carmine screamed.

Carmine, Cole, and Harvey were all being pushed up against Jake and Mikey. It was like there was a wall closing in behind them.

"Ow!!! You're squishing me!!!" Mikey complained. He was pressed between the pile of boys and Serpy's behind.

"None of us can move. The current is too strong!" Cole yelled, trying not to panic. The pressure from the river current trying to flow into the tunnel was growing by the second. And Serpy was still kicking frantically, pushing the boys from side to side and up and down all at the same time. It was getting harder and harder to breathe and it was impossible to control where they were moving.

"It's gonna blow!" Jake yelled just as Serpy's foot made contact with the tunnel wall.

Serpy pushed against the tunnel with all his strength and the boys went flying through the river channel. It was like they were being shot from a cannon into a swirling, twirling, lumpy tube. They were spit out into Lake George before they even realized what had happened.

Mikey finally finished tumbling and was floating just above the lake bottom on his back. "I think I'm gonna throw up." His head, arms, and legs were hanging down from his life jacket and resting on the sandy bottom. He looked like he was performing a magic trick.

"No kidding. I think I did about fifty somersaults in there," Harvey moaned, holding his head and trying to walk straight.

"You must be joking. That was awesome. It was better than riding a ten-foot wave!" Jake said, rubbing his hands together. "I gotta find a way to get my board down here." He headed over to Mikey and pulled him, standing him up.

"I can't believe that my arm is still attached," Cole complained, rubbing his arm with his free hand. "Carmine, we have to find you your own stone. I can't take holding your hand anymore."

"I know. My arm feels like a pipe cleaner. Look." Carmine held onto Cole with his good hand; as he shook his sore arm around and around, it wobbled in circles in the water. It looked like a wet noodle.

"My mom's gonna flip. Look at you guys," Cole said, shaking his head back and forth, looking at his two cousins. Mikey had cuts all over his arms and legs. Carmine's arm was quickly turning black and blue. He looked down at himself. His shorts had ripped when they got caught on something in the tunnel. He was lucky that he had tied his swim shorts string to his fairy stone necklace. At least he still had his shorts and the journal, despite the big rip and the red welt on the back of his neck, which was really starting to sting. He untied the shorts string and rubbed his neck.

All of the boys looked at one another and themselves. Every one of them was scratched and bruised. Serpy watched. He hung his head and started to swim away.

"Hey, wait a minute. You're not home yet. You can't give up on us, we'll still get you there," Mikey called.

Serpy stopped, bent his head, and took some leaves off a stalk of some sort of water lily. He returned to the boys and dropped the pile of green leaves in front of them.

Carmine looked at Serpy with his inquisitive eyes, smiled, and picked up a leaf. "Thanks." Again, Carmine seemed to be able to understand Serpy. He rubbed the slimy leaf on his arm. The bruises immediately began to fade.

"No way. That's so cool, let me try," Harvey said, picking up a leaf and rubbing it on his scratched arm. The scratch disappeared.

"Let me have some too," Jake demanded, grabbing some leaves.

All of the boys used the leaves to heal their wounds. Mikey even rubbed it on his belly, making his queasy stomach feel better.

"Thanks, Serpy. That was a great idea." Cole patted Serpy's head. "Now we'd better get you home, you must be starving.

Serpy nodded his head and as if on cue, his huge stomach rumbled.

CHAPTER 11
LAKE CHAMPLAIN

The river channel leading from Lake George to Lake Champlain was very close to the exit from the Sacandaga channel.

Loony led the way. The whole group was exhausted and moving slowly. Mikey was riding on Serpy's back again and Harvey was taking a turn holding Carmine's hand. They were happy to be out of Sacandaga Lake and away from the worries of news cameras and the carnival.

When they arrived at the entrance of the channel, it was clearly labeled "To Lake Champlain" and it was plenty big enough for Serpy. The current heading into the channel was very strong. It was so strong that they already felt it pulling at them before they even got close.

"Serpy, you'd better go first," Harvey suggested. "We wouldn't want you to get stuck again. But I think this time we'll make sure you're through before we follow you."

"Sounds like a plan. What do you think?" Cole asked the big sea serpent, who looked down with his huge eyes at all of the kids.

Serpy nodded his head up and down and gently set Mikey down on the ground. He nuzzled his nose into Mikey's hair, turned, and swam into the river channel. Just as his tail was disappearing and Harvey and Carmine were getting ready to follow, Mikey screamed. The boys turned around and saw Mikey pointing to a black jellyfish coming out of the Sacandaga channel.

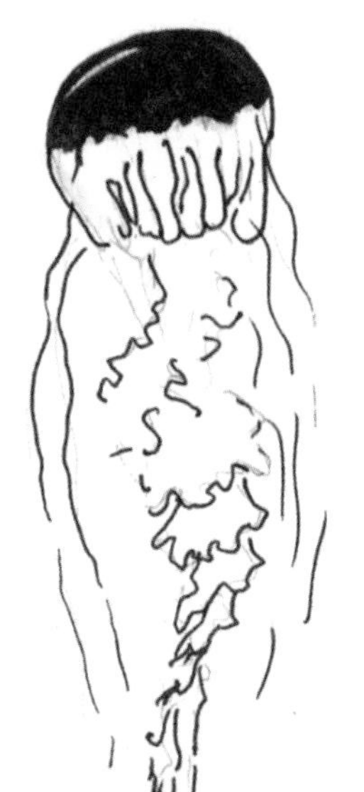

"Quick, everybody in before it sees us!" Cole screamed, pushing Harvey and Carmine toward the channel current. He took Carmine's free hand and reached for Mikey. "Mikey, give me your hand!"

Carmine dug his heels in and pulled his hand free from Cole. "Wait, black jellyfish are afraid of tuna. Tuna, sharks, and some sea turtles are the only predators to the jellyfish. Look, I brought a tuna sandwich in case I got hungry." Carmine yanked a soggy tuna fish sandwich out of his shorts pocket. Blue Dog watched from the other pocket, holding his long fingers over his wide nostrils. "I'll just rub the tuna all over the channel wall and he will be too scared to come in after us."

"Gross. That's gnarly man. I mean, like, that's truly disgusting," Jake said, holding his nose as he watched Carmine smear the tuna fish on the stone walls of the channel opening.

"Here give me some," Harvey said, taking some of the sandwich with his free hand and helping to spread it on the walls.

"I think he sees us! He's coming! Come on. Hurry, Hurry! Let's go!" Cole screamed again, swimming toward the group, grabbing Mikey's arm and Carmine's free hand. He swam, dragging them and Harvey into the tunnel.

"Wait for me!" Jake screamed, swimming into the tunnel and taking Mikey's other hand just as the current sucked them in like a vacuum.

The boys held on for dear life, not wanting to get lost in anymore unfamiliar lakes, especially if the tuna didn't work and the black jellyfish followed them. The channel flowed like a huge raging river, tumultuous waves turning them over and over so they no longer knew which way was up.

Loony swam down and began pushing Cole's feet up so he was facing forward, sitting on top of the current. Cole quickly realized that he could just sit and ride on top of the current. It was kind of like that river log ride at Adirondack Water World.

"Put your feet forward, to the top of the current!" Cole yelled to the others.

Carmine and Mikey put their feet up and sat forward

with Cole.

"Put your feet up!" Mikey and Carmine yelled to Jake and Harvey at the same time.

They all held hands and rode through the long channel on top of the current. They were deposited on the rocky

bottom of Lake Champlain, right at Serpy's feet. The lake had the same greenish tint that seemed to follow Serpy.

"Now, *that* was a better way to get through the channel," Harvey said, standing up and patting Cole on the back. "Nice one, man."

"Yeah, nice, but on the way back, I'm meeting you on the other side. I bet I could have stood on that current if I wasn't holding Mikey's hand." Jake softly punched Mikey in the arm. "Maybe I could teach you to surf and you could ride the river channels with me."

Mikey's big eyes grew to twice their normal size. "Really, I can keep this and come back here again?" He held onto Grace's fairy stone.

"Sorry, you're gonna have to find your own stone, dude, „cause Grace is definitely gonna want hers back," Jake laughed. "And you don't want to upset Grace."

"Wow, my own stone. Wouldn't that be great, Serpy? I could spend every day with you." Mikey climbed back up on

Serpy and reached his small arms around the huge neck. "I'm going to look for one as soon as we get back to camp."

Serpy nodded his head just as an enormous rumble came from his tummy. It was so loud that it actually made little green waves flow away from his stomach.

"Well, Serpy, this is home. Do you think you can find your mom?" Cole asked as Loony, Coolcat, Tink, and Blue Dog all swam around Serpy saying their good-byes.

A low whalelike sound followed by a sharp high-pitched yelp came from farther out in the lake. Serpy's head shot straight up; his tiny ears listening intently. He made a matching low humming sound.

"Is that your mom?" Harvey asked as the sound returned again, a pitch higher this time.

Serpy shook his head up and down. He was so excited that his whole body was shaking.

"Good-bye," Mikey hugged Serpy again. "You're my best friend."

Carmine looked Serpy in the eyes and silently hugged his enormous leg.

Jake stepped up and used his best California surfer accent. "Like, I hope to see you again, dude. Maybe next time you could let me have a ride." Serpy slowly lowered his head and looked up at Jake. "And then maybe you could plug another tunnel and I could surf the wave. Yeah man, that would be like righteous, dude."

Serpy smiled and vigorously nodded his head, knocking Jake back with the waves.

"Oh, I'll be there for that," Cole agreed, giving Jake a high five.

"Count me in too!" Harvey said, joining in.

"Now that we know how to get here, we'll come back to visit. I would say for you to visit us, but you would never make it through the river channels leading to our small lakes." Cole held out his hand to shake with Serpy. Serpy, not sure what to do, offered his webbed foot and shook like a dog would.

"Nice to meet you, Serpy. See you soon," Harvey said, taking the other webbed foot.

Serpy nuzzled his huge head up against Carmine and Mikey and then he looked at all the boys. He blinked back the tears that were beginning to well in his big, yellowy-green eyes. He turned, called to his mother, and swam off into the lake, only looking back once. The boys could all see how excited he was to go home.

CHAPTER 12
HEADING HOME

After Serpy left, they took a minute to look around. Lake Champlain was a huge lake and the boys could tell that it was a place that they would want to visit again. It was tons deeper than all of the other lakes too. The surface was packed with boats, and the houses that they could see through the surface were big and beautiful. And there were signs pointing to different places, like the Dakotis Club, Sprite Slide World, and Under Richelieu River Rapids. And there were signs pointing to the Atlantic Channel and the Great Lakes via Fleuve St. Laurent, and Hudson Bay via Riviera

des Outaouais. They would definitely be coming back here.

"Cole, I'm kinda hungry. Can we go back to camp now?" Mikey asked, pulling at the hole in Cole's shorts.

"Yeah, in a minute, but I'd better write this stuff down. Grace and Julia are never going to believe this." Cole put his hand right down the back of his swim shorts and pulled out the journal.

"Seriously, dude, in your pants? That's where you've been keeping it? I thought you lost it," Jake said, shaking his head back and forth. "But I guess that explains the square butt. I thought maybe you had Spongebob syndrome," Jake laughed.

"I couldn't lose it. We wouldn't know where to go. It's not like I had a lot of choices." Cole opened the journal and began copying everything from the signs.

A group of merpeople gracefully swam out of the channel in front of the boys. They began chattering very quickly in their singsongy voices. They nodded hello to the boys but swam quickly away in the direction of the passage to the Atlantic Ocean.

"Did you hear them?" Harvey asked. "They were talking about the black jellyfish and how the carnival was ruined."

"Yeah, but they said it was captured, a big miracle or something. It was just lying in front of the channel like it was turning itself in. They're bringing it back to the Pacific Council. What do you think that means?" Cole asked. "Do you think it was following Serpy?"

"I don't know, but good job munch- I mean Carmine," Jake said, exaggerating the *Car* and the *mine*. "I bet your nasty tuna sandwich saved the day!" Jake patted Carmine on the back.

"I'm just glad they captured it. I didn't want to see him again," Mikey yawned, holding onto Cole's hand.

"Let's just get home. I think we've had enough adventure for one day," Harvey said, turning with Tink and

Carmine to swim into the river channel, as another group of sprites swam out.

They were wearing full-length swimming costumes covered with beads. They had dark hair and that gorgeous dark, dark, dark skin that you just want to touch because it looks so beautiful. One very light-skinned, light-haired merman was with them. Again, they politely nodded hello, but continued on their way deep in conversation in a language the kids did not understand. But they were pretty sure it was about the carnival and the black jellyfish. Harvey turned and watched as they swam away toward the Atlantic Channel.

"That guy looked just like my Uncle Ady," Harvey said, staring after the group.

"Well, dude, I don't know about that, but give you and your sister tails and you would fit right in with the merpeople. I can just see Olivia with a shell top," Jake laughed and elbowed Cole, "bet you'd like that, huh?"

“Come on, let’s go,” Cole said, completely ignoring Jake’s comment, even though he couldn’t help but picture Olivia and Harvey as merpeople. They really did look like they would fit right in.

Cole took Mikey’s hand and they followed Harvey, Carmine, and the animals into the channel tunnel. Jake and Coolcat followed the group, still giggling.

CHAPTER 13
THE GIRLS

"Mikey stole my fairy stone and it worked for him? And Carmine was with you too?" Grace could not believe what she was hearing.

She and Julia had come home from tennis lessons and had not been able to find the boys. When she asked her dad where they were, he told her that the boys had all gone swimming and looked very tired when they got out of the lake. He said he hadn't seen Cole since, but that Mikey had fallen asleep on a beach chair and Carmine was at the candy store with their aunt Marie.

Grace and Julia headed straight for the clubhouse, Carolyn tagged along, talking about their great serves and how the tennis instructor said she had a strong backhand.

“Chill out. We didn’t mean to go so far and see so much. We just planned to meet Harvey and check out the Chain Lakes like we talked about yesterday,” Cole said.

“What do you mean by *go so far and see so much*? Where did you go?” Grace could hardly stay still she was so desperate to know everything.

“Grace, it’s not a big deal,” Cole sighed, taking a deep breath. “Well, actually it was a big deal, but we didn’t plan it that way. Harvey just wanted to show us around the Chain Lakes. It’s not my fault that Carmine saw a frog and that Mikey followed us with your stone. And it’s certainly not my fault that he went and got lost in Sacandaga Lake.”

Carolyn, who had never been in the clubhouse before, was wandering around checking everything out not really paying attention to the conversation.

Grace reached down to pick up the notebook but Cole grabbed it first, opened it to the back, and handed it to her. “Check it out, I already wrote it all down for you.”

"Wow, this must really be good if you actually wrote all of this. I'll just add my notes to yours," she said. She looked at Julia and then back to the boys. "We're listening."

"We left the dock to find Harvey, but Carmine saw a frog and you know how he loves frogs, so I held his hand and we followed the frog, and it worked. He could breathe underwater as long as he held my hand. He held that frog nearly the whole time, even named it. You should have seen Blue Dog's face when Carmine finally let him go," Cole laughed, remembering how the frog seemed to inflate like a balloon after he was finally free. "But then we headed toward the river channel."

Jake jumped in. "That's when I turn around and like, Mikey's right there, swimming at the bottom of the lake with us." Jake continued telling the girls about meeting up with Harvey and losing Mikey.

"Wait a minute, did you say Sacandaga Lake? But that's where the sea serpent has been," Grace blurted out.

"I know, I know, just listen." Cole continued, "And there's a town, and in the town..." Grace shook her head back and forth. She couldn't believe what she was hearing. Julia was staring at the boys with her mouth open and eyes as wide as they would go. Chippy was doing the same, but with a half-eaten pretzel hanging out of his mouth.

Carolyn sat on the arm of Julia's chair looking back and forth between the kids, her face all scrunched up. She just couldn't quite work out what to think of this story. "Are you guys all right? I mean, like, you're not making any sense."

Jake ignored her and picked up the story again. "So Mikey said he'd met the serpent." Jake laughed, adding, "We might just see Serpy in the paper, or maybe even Harvey's feet."

"What?!" Grace and Julia asked at the same time.

"Yeah, seriously you guys, what're you talking about?" Carolyn asked. "My brother and a sea serpent, yeah right!" She snorted. She stood up and watched Carmine out the window. He was coming back from the candy store. "I'm outta here, anyway. Enjoy your crazy story. I'm going to get some candy." She stood, shaking her head, drawing circles around her ear with her finger making the cuckoo sign and headed for the door.

The boys told the rest of the story, including the news camera, the barn, getting stuck in the first river channel, the black jellyfish, the merman looking like Harvey's uncle, everything. When they finally got to the part of the story where they arrived back at Pleasant Lake, Grace and Julia were both quiet. They didn't know which questions to ask first.

Grace finally broke the silence, “So, do you think you could take us back to meet him?”

“Totally! Right, dude?” Jake asked, looking at Cole. “Serpy promised me a ride and I can’t wait to surf that river channel wave. It was so awesome. And we might see those mermaids again if they all haven’t left yet. And I want to check out that surf shop, and don’t forget the mermaids. Did I already mention the mermaids?” Jake gazed up toward the ceiling with a dreamy smile.

Cole laughed and added, “Yeah, we can take you there, but I’m exhausted. This time-not-changing thing can really get to you, like jet lag or something. I think we’re going to have to wait until tomorrow.” Cole stretched up his arms and rested his head back in his hands, his smile widening as he closed his eyes.

“How are you planning to keep Carmine and Mikey quiet? You know they’re going to want to tell everyone, if they haven’t already,” Grace worried.

"Oh my gosh. Yeah, I forgot that part," Cole said, smiling. "They don't remember any of it. As soon as I let go of Carmine's hand and took your stone from Mikey, they didn't remember anything. Here it is by the way." He tossed her the fairy stone necklace.

"Yeah, it's like it never even happened. I feel sorry for them. It was so awesome and they don't even remember," Jake said, shaking his head back and forth.

CHAPTER 14
CAMP KIDS AGAIN

"Well, that all sounds scary. I, um, mean, exciting. Yeah, exciting, meeting things like sea serpents and mermaids." Julia forced a smile, pushed her glasses up, and adjusted her blue striped headband that perfectly matched her tennis skirt. "But we're not going today, right? We can't today because we have fireworks and the beach Olympics, and I made a strawberry cheesecake for the bake-off and it looks so yummy." Julia didn't even pause for a breath but kept rambling. "Yes, we are much too busy today to do any of that scary, I mean exciting stuff. I mean it's the Fourth of July and my cousins are coming over and my dad got peanut butter cups for s'mores..."

Grace cut her off, "Okay, Julia, calm down, we're not going today. I'll show you all the maps and we can read more about sea serpents. It's going to be fun, I promise." Grace took Julia's hand. "I can't wait to taste your cheesecake. Is it from your new cookbook?"

"Yeah, do you want to see the recipe? I can show it to you and then I can show you my new pink polar bear, it came in the mail today. We could practice our tennis strokes down on the beach." Julia was beginning to breathe a little easier with each new thought, anything to stop thinking about sea serpents and getting lost in river channels.

"The beach, now you're talking my talk. Let's find your cousins and do some normal swimming, or maybe a game of King of the Dock." Jake rubbed his hands together, planning his strategy.

"You're looking at the king right here, so why bother going to the dock?" Cole taunted, standing up on his chair, his blond shaggy hair looking like a crown with the sunlight streaming through the window behind him. "But we may as well make it official," he said, jumping down and leaping toward the door. "See you there."

Cole and Jake took off out of the clubhouse, running down the dirt road toward their camps, jumping over puddles and roots as they went. Julia headed out the door, Chippy happily following behind. She was talking to herself about all the other recipes that she wanted to try this summer.

"I'll be right there, Julia," Grace called, stopping to tuck the journal, a bigger map, and a few more books under her arm before using the moose key to lock up.

The camp kids headed off toward a normal day in the woods, swimming, building sand castles, and later on enjoying the beach party and fireworks.

But lying in bed that night, they were all thinking of their week as water sprites and of all the amazing things that they had seen and done.

Julia lay in bed breathing deeply, trying to work up the courage to meet a sea monster.

Jake was planning his trip to the underwater surf shop to buy an undersurfboard and that book he saw in the window *Extreme Channel Surfing*.

Cole lay, staring at the ceiling, wondering if they could really cross the Atlantic, trying to remember all the places that he had learned about in school.

And Grace was tracing routes to new places in her mind, memorizing all the new maps, and trying to get her head around the fact that there were real mermaids and sea serpents in the lakes in the Adirondacks.

Carmine and Mikey were already asleep, dreaming of sea serpents, watery rollercoasters, and secret entrances to Atlantis.

When the camp kids all finally dozed off, they would all dream of the adventures still to come.

Also available:

campkidsbooks.com